The Trump Satyricon

Petronius Juvenal

Mienmymaw Pubs.

It's fiction, ok?

To the 75 million people who voted for
Kamala and are wandering around going,
'What the hell happened?'

The Trump Satyricon

We all knew it would work against us one day. Our only hope was we could outrun it, or postpone it continuously so as to mitigate the eventual repercussions. But we could not escape it. And now we are paying the price of our subservience to Trump.

Even in 2025, as we were applauding the quick and aggressive stripping away of all Biden radical lib elements from government, society, and culture, and even though in some cases these moves went against all our values, our better judgement, we were emboldened and encouraged. But there was that little click in the back of the brain; we would pay dearly for this.

I was trying to discuss this rationally yesterday with MTG, but she is still adamant that we were in the right, Trump was our destiny. Everything was fair game once Trump put all the pieces in place -the judiciary, military, law enforcement, immigration, the entertainment industry, the global economy, international relations- once he got the rest of the world in a headlock, just by dint of the fact he was actually able to do it, made everything okay. It was destiny. It was our right.

But, was it right?

There were no back rooms where deals were brokered, no secret society, we didn't sneak around hiding motives and intentions, all our cards were on the table. Go ahead, Trump this! And now, we're paying for it.

As they led her back to her cell in the women's correctional facility, all I could think of was that moment in the Chamber, Empty G, as she is now known, all dressed in white, crying out gleefully as Biden fumbled through a mind-numbingly nonsensical State of the Union address, she cried out, 'Liar!' Oh, how we exalted at that moment.

We laughed. We turned our heads to see her up there, crooked mouth, wicked joy in her eyes, crying, 'Liar,' to the President of the United States. We knew the tide was turning and we were going to ride it out for all it was worth.

If Empty G didn't see the end coming, or didn't believe it would come, it wasn't because she was delusional. It was ultimate Trumpian self-assurance. We couldn't be stopped.

Even for those of us who knew the tide would turn, as it always does, the thrill of those early moments was just too exhilarating. I remember the moment when Trump was shot. We, the Players, were huddled at Old Ebbitt's discussing our strategy if Trump were to lose the election, as it appeared he was trying his utmost to do, when the news landed. We stood around glaring at our phones, when suddenly it occurred to me, and I shouted, "It was an illegal! Just watch. Trump's got the election locked up!" Everyone hooted and cheered. It turned out the assassin was not just a bad shot, but a white kid, and far from being an illegal, lived just down the street with his parents, Ozzie and Harriet. Just another screwed up kid, as likely to shoot Biden, Mother Theresa, or anyone else as Trump. But that didn't diminish our exuberance.

What a moment of glory! Triumph! From then on, a bloody-eared Trump could do no wrong. He could dance like a drunken uncle for 39 minutes while a bewildered audience looked on. He could lie bald-faced about illegals eating pets, and Antifa ransacking government buildings, or anything else -repeatedly- anything that could be easily proven false. He drove the fact-checkers crazy. They couldn't keep up. It was a game of whack-a-lie. By time they had exposed one, they were chasing after ten more lies. It was a brilliant -not strategy, Trump's brain is not wired for strategy- but a brilliant ploy. Like cheating at golf.

Jorge has come to take me into the yard. "Ay, amigo," he says, "time to stretch those white legs of yours. What, do you shave those little sticks? Look like a hairless chihuahua!"

No, I'm just old. And you *peso*-ante radicals making us wear shorts, just to humiliate us, doesn't help.

The walk of a thousand steps along the Hallway of Shame, where a large percentage of us are stored, stinks of urine, mold, and mouse feces. The faces glare out at me as I pass. I am among the first allowed out.

In the yard, the grim whirls of barbed wire, with razor edges, the towers, the twenty-foot brick wall, the soldiers standing around idly, with fingers gently tapping the triggers of their automatics as they chat in Spanish with their fellow guards, is our new Senate Chamber. This is where we congregate. This is where we legislate. This is where we slowly disintegrate.

And there's our distinguished speaker. Mitch is in a grumpy mood. He had a particularly tough time with the 'transition.' He tried to ride the fence. Stand up to Trump where it didn't matter, where even Trump didn't care. It made him look tough to the outside world. It made him look, he thought, independent, but all the while his nose was firmly up

Trump's rump like everyone else. Inside, he was a shriveling wuss and he knew it. So long as he played to his constituency, he was untouchable, and he almost got away with it. But de-fanged, he slid down the fence of razors. Mitch was one of the first to go down.

And now old, withered, with no constituency to buoy him up, but still spiteful and unrepentant, he shuffles along the edges of the walls, growling to himself and anyone he confronts. Except the guards. He tries to cozy up to them. He even attempts to speak Spanish to them. Ted tells the story that Mitch asked a guard for '*agua*' and the guard said, 'you know *agua* means dog shit, right?' And Mitch got all confused and started crying. We got a good chuckle out of that.

JD, fucking hillbilly idiot, is standing in the center of the yard lecturing. No one is listening. If Trump were silver and gold, JD was excrement. Everything he said, in his feeble attempt to mimic, placate, impress Trump came out a donkey's ass. If we stood in the glory of Trump, we slunk away from the muck of that monkey hand-puppet.

Shouldn't that, his choice of VP, have alerted us, told us to look a little closer at what was going on, tap the brakes a bit? No, at least we didn't think so at the time. Another Trump whimsy. JD was mouthier than Fly-on-the-Pence, but just as useless. You learn to deal with the idiosyncrasies.

Now, he's going on about the Second Coming. Does he have a new couch? Or is it the glory of the Lord's return? Or the rising up again of Trump. That's a long gone dead deal. No, JD sees a new kind of society arising, one based on some imaginary army of no-bots, people suffused with the literal DNA of Trump to do their bidding. Maybe he's thinking of an army of flesh-eating Minions. I don't know. Pathetic mass of human flesh.

As he drones on, from the other side of the wall a shrieking voice cries out, "Liar!" A couple of us chuckle, but it's more of a painful, not a nostalgic laugh. Good ole Empty G.

For those who study history, we understand the kind of circular series of events that follow a predictable or inevitable course. In recent American history, at least since or with Nixon, the pendulum simply swings back and forth; people get stupid, then they get smart, then lazy and forgetful, then alert and adept, then bonehead stupid again. Then Trump. Throughout history there have been tsunami moments, unpredictable, impossible to prepare for, and these are the moments that alter the course of civilization forever. Christ on the Cross, the Reformation, the American Revolution, the Internal Combustion Engine, The Great Depression, the Cha-Cha-Cha, and alas, Hitler.

And Trump. I want to emphasize the difference between those loyal to Hitler and those beholden to Trump. Yes, they were both narcissistic megalomaniac dictators, but Hitler built a machine of efficient geniuses to carry out his plans, evil though they may have been, whereas Trump surrounded himself with a bunch of idiots. It was always about Trump, and no one else. It's nearly certain he suffered the carnival of idiots because it made him look, in the aggregate, sane. If his little buddy EVlon tried to be Trump's right hand DOGE, he came off more like a half-assed Circus Clown. O, we got a couple laughs with the chain-saw thing, but he was rogue, and had to go.

Then there was RFCK Jr. It should have been cause to rejoice, a major figure from the opposition party defects to your side. Especially in this case. A Kennedy! The lineage, the Dynasty! John, Bobby, Ted- leftist Royalty, and now he's on our side! And what did we get? The Lizard Man who eats his own grandchildren. Even crazy seemed normal around him.

You couldn't hear it, but 'Would you please take him back!' was on everyone's lips.

There's no need to go down the roll-call of the rest of the Stupids, those who created a slurry of confusion and anger with everything they did and said. But we, those of us beholden to Trump, depended on his popularity alone to bolster ourselves up. Let the rest of the dummies go off on their tangents, we had a government to revamp, we had liberties to shore up. We hung in there with Trump because we could increase and maintain our own personal power through him while securing the underpinnings necessary to keep the movement alive. Our Dynasty! We weren't there to blindly do his bidding, he had his Stupids for that. It was only when it all came unraveled -which in no small measure was the doing of his Stupids- that we tried to scurry away. But it was too late. The pendulum swings. And in the end, none of us could say, 'Boy, I didn't see that coming.'

Tucker is in the cell next to mine. He keeps tapping on the wall between us. I think he's trying to communicate with me in some kind of code. I finally yell to him, "Hey Stupid, why don't you talk to me through the bars. I'm two feet away." All I hear is a flurry of tapping on the wall. If anyone wonders how the house of bricks came tumbling down around us. Take a look. The Stupids.

Trump's Tit-for-Tat Tariff wars were annoying, though none of us got too worked up over it. That was his gamble, let him live or die by it. But why Canada? They were by far our largest, most reliable trade partner. They're our next door neighbors! It's not like they left their dog outside barking all night. Why Trump decided to go all Rasputin on them, I don't know. Levying stiff tariffs, threatening annexation, holding them upside down by the ankles, shaking them for spare change. Canadians responded by yanking American wine off their shelves. No more Ernest and Julio, it was all Hoser Red now. They even elected a socialist to get back at us. And then threatened to shut off the electricity to Michigan. Vacationers stayed away from the US in droves, instead, taking their holidays in Iceland. They also gleefully welcomed with open arms all those late night comedians, political cartoonists, celebrity chefs, who got fired or canceled by Trump. They became known as the new 'Draft-Dodgers.' Canada even created a comedy show, 'Late Night with the Draft-Dodgers,' all anti-Trump, of course.

In retaliation, Trump threatened more tariffs. Canada responded as only they can, politely, calmly, 'I'll see your 50%, and raise you 75%.' They had plenty of Tat.

We have been joined by the ghost of Horrors past, our old 'friend,' The Miller. He walks among us, and we're not certain if it's the real person or just a hologram. Every now and again he just suddenly appears. It might be his AI version, or the body corporal. With his vacant eyes, expressionless, emotionless face, his stiff, robotic movements, as if he were born without bone or tissue, there's little difference. And when his lips do move the sound is out of sync with the image. Like a bad live TV feed. Today he seems to float by as an apparition, it is only when he passes JD, and appears to roll his eyes, that we think maybe it is his corporal presence. Which doesn't make us feel any more at ease. He was Trump's Goebbels, his 'intellectual' henchman, and the most feared of all his Stupids. Because the last thing you could accuse The Miller of was stupidity. Pure evil, yes. Stupid, no. We avoid him at all costs.

As long as everyone else around Trump was getting rich, either in prestige, real money, or Bitcoin, they remained happy. Not just happy, they were living in a dream world, where everything was theirs for the taking, like plucking candy from a tree, just reach up and take it. See, the thing is, you didn't have to kowtow to him, all we had to do was outwardly, if not ostentatiously, at least pretend to agree with him. 'Sure, Greenland would make a good 51st State, we ought to take a look at that.' 'Gaza, a resort, with a casino? It's a good thought.' 'Annex

Canada? Sure, look what they're doing with it. Nothing.'

In Nazi Germany silence was the response to the horror, in Trump's America, it was a 'whatever' shrug. It's all fine. The dream could live on forever.

Every day it seems we get a new one. The tribunal has been very active. First, The Miller, and now, U-Hawley. He's brought some comic relief to the yard. Right now he's off talking to himself, plainly disturbed. He's been mocked relentlessly, not just by us, but also the guards. All it takes is for someone to walk past him in grim determination, then turn and give him the big Jan. 6 salute. Everyone cracks up. Not U-Hawley.

I can tell he's pissed, so I sidle up to him. "What's the problem," I say, pretending to be his therapist, "that was your big moment."

He looks down on me, he's tall, and pretty much looks down on everyone, "I'm not a meme," he snaps.

No? It could be worse. How about you sprinting through the corridors of the Chamber like a chicken with its head cut off, trying to escape the very people you were just saluting. That's a good meme.

But, "O come on," I say, "let them have their fun."

He looks down his long snout at me with disdain.

I shrug, okay, be a crybaby. I start to step away, and just to needle him, do a little half-salute, not quite a fist, just a baby salute. He turns away in disgust. I don't think he appreciates the gesture.

The first time someone yelled at the president, "What the fuck are you talking about?" was during a press conference, when Trump boasted that he was the one who drove the snakes out of the Blue Mountains. The second time was at a rally in Des Moines, when he insisted soy beans grew on trees, and "What the fuck are you talking about..." rang out. Probably some old farmer. The third, was when a late night comedienne ran a clip of Trump claiming deodorant caused skin cancer, and she stared at the camera and hissed, "What the fuck... etc." That's when we knew it was a Thing. The WTFers.

We traced their origin back to a WAPO reporter known for his hatchet-job articles questioning Trump's veracity. He railed against his editors in an online rant accusing them of cutting and watering down his more vicious comments; "Quit dancing around with finesse and politeness," he complained. "Attack the bastard. Beat the shit out of his stupidity. When he says something insane, demand, 'What the fuck are you talking about!'" The rant went viral, and soon reporters, TV comedians, and those sham online self-appointed Influencers, Podcasters in their mother's basement, were all shouting out -in print or person –'What the fuck are you talking about?' at just about everything Trump said. Whether flippant or false.

Trump would have his revenge. He had friends. One of them, that arbiter of good taste in America, Bozos, fired the viral reporter, saying 'he crossed the line.' The ever elusive line. And the TV comedienne? She's now doing stand-up in Canada. They're still looking for that farmer in Iowa.

No one did revenge and retaliation better than Trump. He hit hard, and he hit fast. It was brutal, but thrilling. He renamed the Department of Justice (DOJ), the Hammer of Justice (HOJ), and directed Bam-Bam Bondi to investigate anyone who ever done him wrong, was currently doing him wrong, or might in the future do him wrong. Prosecutors were prosecuted, institutions were sued, corporations buckled under his demands. He leaned on the FCC to fire, harass or cancel anyone in the media who was outspoken against him, especially comedians, who were feasting on Trump. Except Kevin Hart, he liked Kevin Hart. Of course he had his ICE goons for roughing up anyone not quite white enough. The MAGA influencers and Foxump News were at his beck and call to attack opponents ideologically -and I use that term very loosely here. And of course, SCOTUS was there to uphold everything Trump did. He would routinely ask, "Don't we have something on that guy? I wanna get rid of him."

We often did.

At the time it felt good to get our revenge. And certainly understandable from our point of view, as we were fed up. For decades, we watched as all our beliefs and actions were debunked and denounced, and everything was taken from us. They came after our guns, tore down our statues, shamed us for being white, pushed us aside to let the Ladies go first, made us stand down while minorities and immigrants got privileged, and then for the sake of less than one-percent of the population, made us remodel bathrooms and change the very language we speak. Our normal way of life was being Canceled. It was time to take out the Big Magic Marker and do a little Canceling ourselves.

Geetz calls me over. He's squatting, drawing diagrams with one finger in the dirt. He says to me only barely moving his lips, "There's going to be a jailbreak tonight," fortunately I haven't lost enough of my hearing to not make out what he says.

"Have you been practicing ventriloquism?" I say, moving my lips.

"Shhh," he hisses, "they're watching!"

I cover my mouth, pretend to cough, "Okay. Jailbreak, you want me to steal a spoon, and dig a tunnel out of here?"

"No," He mumbles, "we're going over the wall."

"Good plan, Einstein," I say, "right into the women's facility."

He looks alarmed, raises his head and looks at the wall, "Not that wall," but he forgot his ventriloquist voice, "O shit, they can lip-read," he says, throwing a hand over his mouth, himself pretending to cough.

Geetz hasn't been looking too good since he lost access to Brylcreem. His hair forks up in dried, dead shrubs, and his forehead seems abnormally stiff. His eyebrows don't move. O. That.

"How'd you manage to get Botox in here?" I say, feigning a sneeze.

He looks around right, left, "I know someone," he says, lips not moving. He actually would make a pretty good ventriloquist, if he weren't such a dummy.

"Well in any case, good luck…." I say, but he grabs my arm, jerks his head to the right, I follow the jerk and see a guard headed our way with a concerned look on his face. He says something in Spanish, I get none of it, but Geetz must know a bit of Spanish, as he says something to the guard, who nods, satisfied that everything is okay, and walks off.

"He wanted to know if we needed a cough drop," he says. "I told him it was just the dust."

We each put a hand to our mouth and cough together in solidarity.

The Constitution opens with, 'We the People.' Trump hated that. Even more so when a certain crowd, political wonks, ex-operatives, and some turncoat past associates of Trump, formed a coalition, calling themselves 'We the People.' They delighted in utilizing the Constitution as a cudgel against our policies. Every time Trump torpedoed a Venezuelan drug-dealer boat, or an ICE agent snatched a mother away from her kids, or when we accidentally deported someone who probably deserved to be deported anyway, there was someone shouting 'due diligence,' or 'first amendment!' The Constitution is pretty vague and wide-open to broad

-shall I say it- liberal interpretation. No where does it specifically say 'thou shall not blow-up a drug-dealer's boat.'

The We the Peepers, as we called them, held rallies, mostly in sanctuary cities, and garnered enough traction to go big-time, with a high profile, nationally promoted demonstration, 'We The People…Not You the King.' Tens of thousands of protestors, demonstrators, radical leftists, Antifa, drug-dealers, flooded every major city, and some very small ones, across the country, waving the Constitution like a hanky, denouncing ICE, SCOTUS, and MAHA-ha-ha. Trump looked down on them like Darth Vader from his Death Star, ready to pounce.

Ted was allowed out of solitary confinement today. He stands in the center of the yard strapped to a pole, our tether-ball pole, his hands bound behind his back. His beard is long and scraggly. He is brought out every now and again so that he can repent before all of us. And to entertain the guards.

He is spouting his usual gibberish, "I'm just here on vacation, I asked my daughters, it's school break, where do you want to go? Mexico, Mexico they both cried…yes, yes, good idea, so here we are on vacation, lovely Mexico…"

A guard shouts out, "This isn't exactly Puerto Vallarta!"

"I love Mexico," he hollers joyously.

Poor Ted, that's what he gets for crossing Trump, on one little -but to Trump- very crucial issue. Ted had the audacity to say on his Podcast that Trump should not be involved in the firing of comedians just for criticizing him. It's free speech, it's in the Constitution. Well, Ted found 'the line,' and crossed it. It put him outside the box, and once you're outside that Trump Box, you're open to attack from both sides. He's been in repentance mode ever since. For everything. The other day he apologized for the Spanish Inquisition. Now he raves on, explaining how his luggage got lost, and he ended up here. It gets tedious after a while.

My mind wanders. I pass by Geetz who whispers, "Jailbreak tonight… pass it on," and is gone.

I squat in the dust. Put my head in my hands. I still can't believe it.

Among all the unnecessary distractions that sent our Jenga-like structure crashing down, was Crypto. Trump took a deep dive investing in Cryptocurrency, forming his own Non Fungible financial company, with memecoins, stacked trading algorithms, blockchains, and market manipulations, 'buy the dip!' He single handedly created a bullish Bitcoin market. He was worth millions! In play money. And if the boss can do it, FOMO, everyone from the lowest House intern to the highest cabinet members wanted in. The big banks, public companies, tech-industry, hip-hop moguls, my crazy cousin Jimmy, everyone hopped happily on board the Good Ship Crypto. Except me.

Oh, I pretended to be heavily invested. When standing around gabbing in Blowbart's office, an Old Fashioned in hand, I'd crow, 'Oh yes, I'm up seventy-percent since last week.' And someone would top me with a one-hundred-five percent increase. We all chuckled heartily. Wasn't it great? We were all getting rich on make-believe money.

But Trump held all the cards. He was using Real World Assets against his financial entities, hiding Crypto money -in plain sight. These were used to fund several of his pet projects, like his new mansion at Mar-a-Lego, a multi-million ballroom. For security purposes. Just as he had done with the courts, the deck was stacked, everything was arranged to protect and benefit himself.

Didn't we see that he was in it for his own gain? Of course we did, it was too obvious, but playing along was part of our strategy. Trump was invincible. Trump was money. We could play along, from the sidelines, siphon off every bit, or enough, of what we needed. If the rug got pulled out, we had safety nets. Didn't we? We would find out when the pieces came tumbling down.

Jorge said something weird to me this morning, jokingly, "Your English, very good, where'd you learn to speak such good English?" He was smiling in such a way that made me think he might be familiar with the reference. Or was he? It was one of those Trump moments, right up there with his takedown of that little Gecko from Ukraine. In this case, he openly belittled the President of Liberia, where the official language is English, repeatedly asking him how he spoke such good English. Some libs took it for blatant racism. I don't know, I thought he was just being inquisitive. Did Jorge know about this incident? Or, just coincidence?

I want to ask him, or allude to it somehow, as we walk the corridor of shame, but the sudden sight of a new inmate shocks me. It's Hogspit, one of the Top Stupids who brought down the house of cards. He's clutching the bars as we walk past, with an ugly look on his face. I purposely turn my head away as we pass on, but he won't let it go, "Traitor," he snarls, "scum. When the revolution comes you're going to be the first to go."

Jorge stops us, looks at the pig, "You missed it, bro, the revolution came and went, and look where you are."

We continue our walk.

When Trump demanded Mexico erect a series of detention centers along the border, I don't think this is what he intended. Since his first term Big Beautiful Wall never got more than a couple map-inches long, and was porous as hell, for his encore second term he came up with the grand idea of getting Mexicans to build detention centers all along the border, and when illegals were caught, stuff them in the convenient jail, and be done with them. Immigration problem solved.

Mexico would have nothing to do with it. Trump threatened to cut aid to them by 134 % (I've tried to do the math, can't be done), more tariffs, even military incursion (blah blah blah). Unimpressed, the Mexican Congress shrugged, "You want detention centers on the border," they insisted, "you will have to pay for them yourself." Trump found -siphoned- money from FEMA and from the Department of Education (after he slid it under the door to become part of the HOJ), and created a budget sufficient enough to build a 'pilot' detention center. Because he's all about America first, he got bids from a number of American firms, all of which came in ten times over the budget. Well, America first, unless there's a cheaper way. Trump went back to Mexico, who looked at the allowance, and said, "If you want us to use American dollars to build it, we'll build it." They built it, now we're in it.

In the yard, a number of us close ranks and discuss the latest developments. I mention Hogspit's presence, and this brings nods and shakes of heads, both signifying the same thing, who's next to join us? They're going higher up the chain, how far can they go? A couple of guards mosey up and motioning with the tips of their automatic rifles, make it clear we need to disburse. "Is it true he's coming here?" One of the less wise guys among us says, with only a hint of sarcasm.

One guard shrugs (we're never sure which ones understand English), "Who knows…you want to be around to find out?"

We disburse.

It all began to unravel when I was on a fact-finding mission in Taiwan. My marching orders were to berate, humiliate, and intimidate the

Professor President of that beleaguered little island. China was intent upon sucking Taiwan into its Commie claws, and had three aircraft carriers and two battleships positioned at key trading ports around the tiny island. Silently, threateningly. Taiwan begged for our help, playing the 'We're a democracy, like you,' card. Well, no democracy is like ours. The Professor was all but in tears when I told him there wasn't much we could do. Trump had a lot of respect for Xi-Xi personally, and didn't want to jeopardize our international relations with another world power. Sorry, Taiwan, you are not a world power.

So, if you want help from us, you're gonna have to pay up. The Professor President, taking the hint, offered a raft of fancy shiny computers with built-in social media access, a gaming console, and all the K-Pop music you could bear. Gratis. (Shipping not included.)

Not quite on par with the $400 mill flying fortress Trump had in his back pocket, from his buds in Saudi Arabia. I told him Trump was more comfortable with tariffs. Computers, we can get anywhere. China, for instance. He then broke down and offered free shipping. I told him, with the sorriest look I could muster under the circumstances, I would relay his offer to the President.

Back home, not surprisingly, sympathy for Taiwan was rampant. I think people had grown tired of the Ukraine thing dragging on forever and needed a new tiny, worthless country to get all worked up and teary-eyed about. The Taiwanese flag was hoisted on every other house on the block. Tai cuisine was all the rage (which irked Thailand, because Thai -not Tai- cuisine was supposed to be the rage -no piggy-backing allowed!). Sympathy dripped from every social and cultural pore.

The EU, led by France and Germany offered to come to Taiwan's aid, and were joined by England and Canada. What they were doing of course was thumbing their nose at us. Trump had at times shown some disdain for the EU, Canada, Scandinavian countries, South Korea,

Brazil, and on and on, and was not so much appreciated in certain international circles. Taiwan became an international test case.

There was a pause in diplomacy. Then Trump came up with a beauty of a deal, one that would both rattle Taiwan, while offering them a glimmer of hope. It might also aid the US, or at least add some lining to Trump's pocket. I received the directive to tell Mr. Professor President, "We'll give you aid…in the form of cryptocurrency, with which you can use to buy all the arms you need. From us."

Taiwan was notoriously opposed to cryptocurrency, with steep regulations against its use, for anything. I relayed in person the offer to the Professor. He paused an unblinking several moments. "I cannot do that," he said, adjusting the glasses on his nose, "there are laws in this country prohibiting such transactions outside the approved currency."

I leaned forwards, tapped him on the knee, "It's your country," I reminded him, mimicking what I'm sure the boss would have said, "you can do with it whatever you want."

He kept his eyes on me, unwavering, "You have it backwards," he said with a wan smile, "I do what my country wants."

Next day, Trump announced 102 % percent tariffs on most goods exported from Taiwan, all computer hardware, software, ink cartridges, shipping labels, and plastic twisty-ties. But not mangoes, we needed the mangoes.

The tech industry went nuts, because, while none of them knew what a mango was, they really needed those plastic twisty-ties, their whole packaging and shipping operation relied on them. EVlon flew into a rage and announced he was forming a Third Party to combat Trump's revenge-based tariffs, and he would call it the Twisty-Tie Party. I think that lasted two days.

There's a number of jokes going around as to how Mighty Mouse Mike keeps his hair neatly combed, and so slick and shiny in this dusty, flea-bitten place. It ain't Brylcreem. He walks among us pretending he's leading a coalition through the corridors of power, carrying a make believe folder under his arm. He wants to get us in line behind Trump, and only Trump. He is one of those who needed Trump to account for his existence. But he's just pretending. He walks up to me, "I have your vote on the New Improved Big Beautiful Bill, right?"

"You betcha," I say. He nods contentedly, and scribbles a note in his folder, and walks off. He does this several times a day. You got my vote, buddy.

He goes next to Tubby, who's patting the pigskin, getting ready to toss it over the wall to Blowbart. Tubby nods at Mighty Mouse's request. Yup, Tubby's on board, for anything. He hurls the football over the wall, and we hear a loud, "Owww…hey!"

Geetz is standing next to me watching as the Mouse seeks a coalition. "I coulda…shoulda had that job," he says spitefully.

"Why, are you all that good at doing nothing?" I say. And when Geetz smiles, his forehead cracks.

Chicken Tacos does not have a divisive ring to it. Unless you allow it to. We have tacos two or three times a week, but when Jorge says, "Today, chicken taco, just for you," grinning broadly. He's up to something.

I see it right off, in the mess, a large banner over the shoveling table simply reads 'Chicken TACO,' with a cartoonish picture of Trump. Okay. Most of us shrug, the cost of losing. But Paxxy blows up when he spots the banner, and howls out in his Texas accent, "Hey! Are you insulting our leader?" He lifts a taco as if he's going to toss it at the banner. "Bastards! Insulting us, our president, our leader…" chipotle sauce is dripping down his arm. Even the Mexican gals serving the slop are alarmed. "Don't think we don't know what you're doing. Insult! Taco! Chicken taco! I will not eat this shit!"

One guard, who spoke enough English to be humored by his tirade, says, "So take your business elsewhere, senor."

That gets a couple titters, which sets off Paxxy even more, "Our fuhrer does not chicken out!"

At least I think he said 'fuhrer,' it gets kind of noisy in the mess.

Paxxy did a little Texas two-step before the Texas legislature. He was impeached by the State House, overwhelmingly, for some monetary indiscretion, which was blatant and obvious, as he left a paper trail like toilet paper stuck to his shoe a mile long. Even by Texas Politics standards, it was about as openly stupid as could be. But, after a few months dormant period, when ethical senility and cronyism set in, the Senate took up the issue, and overwhelmingly un-impeached Paxxy. He came back meaner, more spiteful, and vengeful than ever.

And then his wife, herself a prominent (Texas State Senate) legislator, caught her good Christian boy cheating on her, big time. Monetary indiscretion is bad, sexual indiscretion, worse. The two together, nuclear. The divorce was ugly, and should have been the end of his career, but this is Texas. And this is Paxxy. He continued playing dirty tricks that would make Nixon proud. The walls only came crumbling down, when he was nabbed crossing the Rio Grande (to inspect this very detention center), with an underage little Mexican hottie. There's an old saying, 'You can't cross the same river twice.' Paxxy certainly didn't.

In the yard, I crouch next to him, because he's still looking pissed off, like he needs to punch someone. "Pretty slick of you," I say, "beating that grift rap."

"Grift?" he spins his head around, glares at me, "there's no such thing as grift. Taking advantage of the situation. That's all it is."

"And your girlfriend?"

Paxxy nods, as if at a pleasant memory. "She was so….fucking hot!" He seems lost in reveries, "But…the Bible says, 'thou probably shouldn't committeth adultery,'" he pauses, "unless…she's hot!" Then laughs. "So, I broke it off."

"Mighty white of you," I say, "you're a good man, Paxxy," I pat him on the back.

He nods. Yes, yes, he agrees, he is a good sort. He walks off nodding pleasantly.

The WTP was gaining more influence, and as their demonstrations became more frequent, more organized, and more scrutinized, Trump took to paying spies, informers, influencers, a handsome sum (in Crypto!), to infiltrate, agitate, and if necessary initiate a tussle. And be sure to record it. They were pretty obvious to spot, with their iPhones at arm's length, MAGA hats, and, 'Here, light off this firecracker, would ya?' It's not the best and the brightest do this kind of work.

But the We the Peepers had their own spies, doing pretty much the same thing, except with weepy empathy. So we had spies spying on spies who were spying on each other until pretty soon at any rally or demonstration all you would see is everyone pointing their cameras at each other.

The WTP had Trump seething inside. Their clamor of 'free speech' and 'due process,' and all those kids walking around in 'We the People' tee-shirts, was enough to drive him nuts. He so wanted to kneecap them, strip them of any power. And that meant undermining the Constitution itself. And he found a way to do it.

He invited himself to speak at a Convention of the ALA (American Librarians Association), held, symbolically, in Philadelphia. He claimed he wanted to address the Librarians to get their 'feedback.' Which is Trump-speak for, 'I'm gonna wup your ass.'

He did not have a good relationship with librarians in general, having fired the Librarian of Congress, for being too DEI (he even said that out loud), and then renaming the Library of Congress, the Library of the President, and appointing himself as Chief Librarian. It figured to be a somewhat contentious speech. Trump doesn't gather people to share recipes.

He took to the podium. After some preliminary puffery, and pot-shots at Biden and the Dems, he took out his copy of the Constitution, dog-eared and ketchup stained as it was, and pretended to pore over it, "The Constitution," he intoned, with grandiosity, holding up the document, "you ever take a look at this thing? I have. It's old, very old, when it was written, what, 100 years ago, 200? It was a beautiful thing, and people really liked it, but that was a long time ago, before Reagan was born. It's got no use anymore." He looked down at the paper, odiously, "Let's see, 'We the People.' What does that mean? What people are they talking about? Illegals? Harvard illiterates? DIY hires? You heard about those? DIYs? We got rid of that. It's a very badly written document. I'm going to write a new one, yeah, a new Constitution, more modern, a beautiful Constitution, no more 'thou shalt nots,' and 'wherefores' and 'whynots,' it'll begin with, 'My people,' cuz that's who it's for, My People. It'll be like a manual for repairing your toaster. Useful. Yeah, you heard it here first, I'm going to write a new Constitution!"

He paused to allow the applause to subside, but as there was no applause, he went for the boffo joke, "You're all so quiet…oh, I forgot, I'm in a libarry…" still no laughter, "so let me ask you, do we really need libraries anymore? They don't make money. You don't sell nothing. People check out books, and don't return them. How much money do you make on late fees…I bet not a lot."

"We don't charge late fees anymore," a white haired, white bearded Librarian said.

"No fees? no wonder you guys are broke, you're costing me a fortune, do you know what the library budget is? I don't know either, but I'm sure it's more than your late fees would make up for, if you were smart enough to collect them…you just give books away for free? That's crazy, that's not how to run a business… how about this, how 'bout we turn all the libraries into bookstores…yeah," he nodded with inspirational glee, "we could make the Library of the President our flagship, I'd go there, so here's what we're going to do…we're going to make all libraries bookstores…what a great idea, and I just thought of it, standing here, see that's why they call me the business genius. These things just come to me. A bookstore. Where people buy books, no more walking out the door with them, and no late fees, let me give you a little business tip…buy low…sell high…you make money. That's how it works, and the first book they'll buy? My new Constitution, in book form, everyone'll want a copy for the whole family, help out the economy…not that we need it, we got the greatest economy in history…did you know that…in one year I made this greatest economy in the world…any questions?"

"Sir, when can we expect this new Constitution to come out, do you have a publication date…?"

"Who's the publisher…?"

"What's the retail price?…"

With all the confidence of a con man, Trump stated triumphantly, "In two weeks, in two weeks you'll have the answer to all those questions… next…"

That little white bearded librarian stood up and asked, "So am I to understand you're the new Librarian in Chief?" Trump nodded, proudly. "So, hey boss, can I get a raise?" The room erupted in cheers and fist pumping.

Trump snapped back, "Once we turn libraries into bookstores…then you can give yourself a raise…"

With that he left the podium. He didn't want to miss his tee-time.

I will admit, off the record, I often got unnerved by some of Trump's stretching of Presidential 'plenary' powers, as his personal Goebbels advocated. Not just the big things, like pissing off the entire world, but I'm thinking more of the, let's just call them, impromptu moments, when he suddenly blurts out he's going put a Strip Joint on the Gaza Strip, or write a new Constitution.

Sometimes I just wanted to say, 'What the fuck are you talking about?' But I kept it inside my head.

JD is standing in the middle of the yard, "It doesn't have to be true," he raises an arm as if he has a pointer in his hand, "I'm making a point." He has a way of uttering things no matter how muddleheaded, with such confidence and sincerity, you stop and think, well, yeah, that makes sense. And then you go, no, wait, that's stupid. "It's not a matter of whether it's true or not," he insists, "I'm making a point. There is no wall keeping you inside. All of these guards, they are the illegals, from

Venezuela, they're the ones being held here, not us. We are the guards, they are the prisoners, come on, they have no guns, no authority, they are the prisoners, ignore them, follow me out the Silver Gates." JD begins marching towards the large gates, which as far as I know do not open, they're composed of barbed wire and rebar, and JD is walking straight at them, "It doesn't have to be true," he cries out, "if you're just making a point," and his forehead and nose makes contact with a point, a very sharp metal one, of the non-existent fence kind, his head jerks back, but he tries stepping forward again, and takes a shot right in the knee, he stumbles, but gets back up.

Tubby drawls in his turtle voice, "You made your point, now quit being a dope, and just stop, before you hurt yourself."

Bleeding from the head, both knees, and palms of his hands, JD turns, smiles, "Point made." He hobbles off.

The guards have been watching this theatrical display with some amusement and not a small amount of alarm, as a couple had even started to approach JD before Tubby stepped in.

See. It's not all lunacy.

'But for the price of eggs, the Kingdom would have remained intact.'

Sounds like a good historical quote, and I want credit for it when historians go sifting through the garbage trying to find clues as to what happened. It was the eggs. If toilet paper was the symbol of the Pandemic, eggs became the symbol of Biden's Inflation. Trump took full advantage in his campaign, promising to lower the cost of eggs on his first day on the job. Well, more than a year into his second term, not only had the price of eggs not come down, they had gone up. And the Podcasting libs jumped all over it. One selfie Influencer recorded himself approaching a store clerk, holding up an egg, "How much for just one?" The clerk shakes her head, sorry.

It was funny. I guess. Short, quick, made its point. That it was filmed in a well-known chain grocery store with obvious leftist leanings (DEI hires!), was obvious to everyone. So Trump took to attacking 'Traitor Joe's' in every speech and in all his Social Outrage Posts. These are the kind of attacks that can backfire.

No-No-Noem didn't help, as she visited chicken farms in South Dakota and actually yelled at the chickens to put out eggs faster and cheaper. Fortunately she didn't shoot any of them. When her entourage stopped for gas, she railed at the attendant for keeping prices too high. The kid looked a bit confused, "I don't get any of that money." She got in her limo, rolled down the window and shouted, "Lower your damn prices." This went over really big with the rank and file. On both sides. The MAGAs cried, "Right on, let's get those prices down." And the left cried "What a fucking idiot, talking to chickens."

About the same time, we lost Ben and Jerry's. You can't expect to win that big chunk of the Center, Main Street America, if you lose the ice cream vote.

I'm trying to roll and fold my 'enchilada,' which looks more like a wad of mushed tortilla with some grayish green goop in the middle, when a voice, like that of God amid a tremolo of angels singing on high, intones, "Fellow prisoners…Hello! Believers…hello! To all the beholden, hello!!" Everyone in the mess stops, looking around for where the voice is coming from, because it has an eerily familiar ring to it, one that sends chills down the spine. It seems not to be coming from speakers, but floats down like fog from a cloud, "Take heart believers, as you labor in Satan's chains…" ah, of course, it's The Miller. His ethereal self brings the smell of sulfur and stinkweed to the mess hall. We look around for something to swat at, as the voice continues, "This is not a time for despair…" it drones, none of us were despairing in any case, we're just trying to get something in our stomachs so we don't faint out in yard, "You, the beholden, the chosen ones, you who have sacrificed your freedom, your liberty, your status and power, you have lost your family, your brave wives back at hearth and home, cooking good ole America grilled squirrel, gone, but you will never be lost to your poor children, or to your children's children, or to the children of your children's children, or…where was I? Oh yeah, your sacrifice will be remembered for thousands of years, your names will be etched in Gold in the Marble Halls of America the Great! For the time is coming, coming soon, that the beast will be awakened, and yay, I say merrily unto thee, that the beast will be the beast of truth, of freedom, the beast of good white people. For remember your lineage, direct descendants of Athens, of Rome, of Berlin, throw off your shackles, you are the chosen few, you will bring your strength, your power, your hidden insecurities, and rise! Rise up with me, brothers, rise, and together with your gray suits and purple ties, throw off the shackles and rise! Go and smite thine enemy, so wicked, so cruel, bunch of weak little faggots and… " we're all standing around with our mouths open, not so much because we are trying to eat, but because we want to know where that damn voice is coming from so we can smack it shut. "Rise Brothers! The time is coming, rise, brothers…and look back on your sisters, down there, look how tiny they are, rise, brothers…you, the chosen heroes of western civilization, rise! The time has come…"

Suddenly there's a loud crackle, a hiss and a buzz, the voice is cut off, and a robo-female voice, equally disembodied and ethereal, takes over, "You have five seconds left on your call…Please insert more coins if you would like continue your call…if not, please hang up after five seconds…"

"I don't have any more coins…goddam it, does anyone have any coins…shit…."

"You now have three seconds…insert more coins if you care to continue your call…"

"Shit…" There's a loud click and the voice fades into oblivion. The line is dead. I lay an extra slice of avocado toast on my tray, and go sit down among the others, equally perturbed and relieved.

When Trump heard the Canadian show 'Late Night with the Draft-Dodgers' had received an Emmy nomination, he went looney tunes. In one of those impromptu moments, in the middle of a rally in Wisconsin hailing the comeback of American cheese, he made a nasty remark about the Draft-Dodgers, then said, "I'm the one who should get an Emmy," he pointed at his audience, "don't you think?…I'm a brilliant showman, everyone says that, 'he's a brilliant showman.' I oughta get an Emmy…" The stunned onlookers bobbled their heads in agreement.

The fact is, he had already had two Emmy nominations for his performance as a President during his first term, and lost out both times to reruns of 'Gilligan's Island.' He hates losing. So he assembled his crack team of Stupids and they put together 'Trump's Biggest!' a two-hour collection of clips from his rally speeches, news conferences, of him taking down that little Ukraine Gecko, telling EU leaders to their face they were idiots, proudly locking hands with Putin, Xi-Xi, Bibi, and MSB, and finally it ends —as it should- with his famous pose with the bloody ear. The 'show' was scheduled to run on FoxRot, but there was a problem. Trump insisted his playlist be used as the soundtrack. The producers scrambled to get rights for all the songs, but only one artist would give his permission, and I don't think anyone wants to listen to two hours of 'Cat Scratch Fever.'

The show was submitted to the Emmy Board, and got a quick reply: 'The category you submitted this for does not exist. Did you want to enter it in the Fantasy/Horror category?'

When the Emmy nominations were announced, 'Trump's Biggest' was nowhere to be found. He went ballistic, tossing ketchup bottles at the bedroom wall, hollering at everyone who crossed his path. At the morning cabinet meeting, JD stood and applauded when he entered, Bam-Bam Bondi cried out, 'Great show, boss, you were cheated!' 'Isn't he a great guy,' L'il Marco cried. 'Hey, you got my Emmy!' Krash said. 'Brilliant work, sir," Hogspit added. At that day's media briefing, Bullet-Lips Leavitt revealed that Trump was demanding the HOJ investigate the National Academy of Television, Arts, and Sciences (NATAS, which runs the Emmy Awards), and in the meantime was taking over as Chief of the Board, replacing the current Board of Governors with everyone in his family.

The radical leftist elites had fun with Trump's dismay, generating a flurry of memes for Trump's next entry for an Emmy; Trump (in a Tutu) on 'Dancing With the Stars,' opposite Rosie O'Donnell. As a contestant on the 'British Baking Show,' wearing a Pru wig and glasses down his nose, with a look of horror on his face when his soufflé goes flat.

I ignore Geetz as much as I can, but yesterday he approached me with a direct command: the escape was planned for that evening, I was to watch the south tower, and at the signal, a shout from Mighty Mike, I was to cause a distraction, he suggested feigning a heart attack. (Do I look like a candidate for a cardiac episode? Apparently.) When they come to give me CPR (yuck!) the cell the guards will be overtaken. "By who?" I said.

"Just do it," Geetz's ventriloquism lessons forgot to mention not to bellow when ventriloquating.

I don't know exactly what happened, but last night I heard a commotion, down the hall. Shouting, some scuffling, then a shot rang out, then two more. Tucker was banging furiously on the wall with both hands.

Then silence. The cell mates along Scum Row began murmuring, then calling out to one another asking what happened. What was going on?

"I think they killed him," someone shouted.

"No…" another said, "he got free, he's out."

"I saw him lying on the floor."

"It was just a dummy!"

"Then that's him all right!"

Puerile guffaws filled the hallway.

And then a band of guards flooded the row, going cell to cell rattling on bars, and shouting orders. Jorge passing my cell said, "You okay?"

"I think I'm having a heart attack," I say, smiling. Hopefully he didn't get the joke.

Mid-terms were lurking in the not-too-distant future, and there was nothing but distractions and unrest, both international and domestic. China had begun bombarding Taiwan with drones, taking out key 7-Elevens and Gua Bao food carts. Ukraine had stretched a wire along its border tripping Russian troops as they entered. A 'blooper reel' of soldiers stumbling around Kharkivi was all over social media. On our own border, Mexican cartels began seizing control of ICE facilities in numerous cities. On the north, Royal Canadians Mounties were stationed at key entry points from Nova Scotia to Vancouver Island. Looking Royal.

California was suffering the worst spate of wildfires in over a decade, destroying major metropolitan areas, causing billions of dollars in damage, and that was just to two houses, and a coffee shop. Trump refused to send FEMA in, claiming, "Fire is good for California, make it a Red State.' In blatant defiance of Trump, Governor Newsance formed a coalition with the other two radical-left lib Blue States to the north, creating the WCA (the Worst Coast Alliance). Claiming States's rights, they established their own S (State)EMA, imposed strict limits on ICE, its facilities and agents, and the National Guard was not allowed entry unless they were sponsored by a friend or family member. The WCA virtually declared themselves a separate entity. Fine with us. As far as we were concerned, you could take an Exacto Knife and just slice off the whole of the West Coast.

I return to my cell, and see Tucker, his ear pressed against the wall, I think waiting for a reply.

I decide to play a game with him. I must be bored. I start tapping against the wall, with a coin, rapping out a code to the rhythm of 'Jingle Bells,' two verses. I wait. There's a flurry of tapping from the other side. It's not 'Jingle Bells,' more like 'The William Tell Overture.' But that's giving the moron too much credit. I reply with an ominous three taps, 'I'm…very…bored.' He replies with two taps, which I translate as, 'me…too.'

The Farmers of California United (FoCU), organized demonstrations against the administration, demanding an end to crippling tariffs that had frozen sales of beet and rutabaga to Belarus, while China refused to buy American soy beans, leaving California and Iowa with enough soy beans to fill Albert Hall. They also demanded an end to immigration policies that were leaving fields rotting because there was no one to harvest the kale, except white people, and we don't do that kind of thing. The protests originated at the Santa Barbara Farmers Market, and expanded to Solvang, then further north up the coast, all the way to Monterey. The high-profile hubbub attracted the attention of WTPeepers, and soon the Central Valley was rife with constant protests, or PRO-tests, as they were advertised.

Then Newsance had a brilliant idea (he said), whip up all this frustration and energy and take your demonstration to Washington, DC. Put together a convoy of tractors, travel cross country to DC, and treat the capital to a very French form of expression by using tractors to blockade 1-495, really cinching up the Beltway. It sounded bonkers, impossible, but right up the alley of muddleheaded Antifa radicals. When they set out from San Luis Obispo with four tractors, a combine, and a couple flatbed trucks, we all laughed; 'they won't make it to the border.' Foxump News, guffawing and making fun, showed old tractors bumping along a two lane highway. By time they reached Nevada they had a convoy a mile long of tractors, harvesters, combines, with farmers and PRO-testers walking alongside. Through Utah and Colorado, Iowa farmers joined in, tossing soy beans to the kids lining the streets. In Kansas they picked up dozens more tractors, and hundreds more demonstrators, farmers walking alongside carrying pitchforks and cornstalks.

From Oklahoma and Arkansas they came, playing banjos, and whistling, dancing and singing. By time they hit Missouri, with the crowds crying, 'Who me? Show me!' The convoy was blocking traffic for miles and hours along I-64, headed for St. Louis, and the Mississippi River.

Trump was enraged. He announced he was going to crush the convoy before it crossed the Mississippi. He sent Heckle and Jeckle, JD and U-Hawley, to man the barricades at the east end of Eads Bridge.

The demonstrators had planned an epic crossing of the Mississippi with a weekend of demonstrations and speeches, live music headlined by Jimmy Thudpucker, dancers, baton twirlers, high school marching bands, and then the hundreds of farmers, immigrants, in lock-step would march ahead of the tractors to the sound and sight of fireworks and cross over the Mighty Mississippi into the East -where most good American citizens live. The National Guard set up on the east side of the river hoping the protestors would be trapped on the bridge, and jump off into the river, maybe hitting Mark Twain on the way down. Newsance had flown out to lead the march across the bridge, and after a rousing speech in which he combed his hair three times, they set out. Eads is a long bridge, and JD and U-Hawley, standing symbolically at the barricades trying to look like the Guardians of Asgaard, unfortunately looked more like just a couple of dweebs standing on a bridge. Trump arranged to have FR-17s screaming overhead, but that just brought more cheers from the protestors, as they approached the east end, chanting, 'We the people…we the people…' and 'We're Illegal and we like it!' 'No farm-to-table tonight!' 'I got your corn right here,' under a banner of a fist with a corn cob poking up as the middle finger.

These particular National Guard recruits were from rural North Carolina, and what they saw coming towards them was not Antifa extremists, but Maw and Paw. With tears in their eyes, they laid down their weapons, broke through the barricade and ran to join the marchers. JD and U-Hawley stood alone, arm and arm to face the crowd bearing down on them, jets overhead, the Mighty Mississippi surging below, and suddenly JD let out a 'Yee-Haw,' and started to race headlong at the protestors, but he tripped over U-Hawley's big foot, and tumbled ass backwards to the cement. As U-Hawley tried to help JD to his feet, he put up his arm to halt the oncoming crowd, but they thought it was his Jan. 6 salute, and they laughed and came racing towards the duo. Tangled up in each other, JD tried to throw U-Hawley to the ground to make his own escape, but fell and then crab-crawled off into the bushes, while U-Hawley broke into a long-legged trot that took him all the way back to DC.

The triumphant Tractor Rebellion rolled on. It was the beginning of the end.

Geetz is strapped to the pole in the center of the yard. His head and eyebrows have been shaved and his bulbous forehead now stands out like a neon billboard in Times Square. His 'escape' was a far more elaborate scheme than I had thought. Geetz had a car waiting for him on the outside, a cherried-out low-ride Cadillac, vintage 1962, filled with four teen-age hotties. He bribed two guards (not Jorge, though I found this out from him) with promises of sexual favors. Geetz with the guards and a couple buddies would exit the compound, jump in the car and whiz off. But the scheme fell apart. Mighty Mike was supposed to yell, "Jailbreak!" and then I was going to collapse on the floor. But he forgot his line, and stood kind of wheezing and whistling, and in desperation yelled, "Geetz is breaking out of jail," and the two compromised guards started to open Geetz's cell, but the other guards saw right away what was going on, and guns fired, Geetz hit the floor… and Mighty Mike finally yelled, "Jailbreak." No one was hurt, except the two liable guards who are now in custody (in Texas).

Not exactly the stuff of the Great Escape. It was that kind of a planning that landed most of us in this shit hole to begin with. Poetic justice?

England and France came to the aid of Taiwan, providing military escorts for ships into blocked ports, freeing up trade, and using anti-drone technology developed in Ukraine, downing and destroying drones. The wounded drones could be seen flopping around in palm trees, and scuffling along sidewalks trying to get air born. China blinked, and while they did not remove their ships from around the island, they called off the drones. For the time being.

Weary American ambassadors around the world were being told to 'pack your bags and go home and worship your false idol.' The unemployment line in DC was growing.

Our ambassador to Taiwan, Barbi, the wife of a Crypto-mogul who mapped the algorithms that made Trump rich, and the rest of us bankrupt, panicked. She thought the Taiwanese were going to kill her. She tried to escape to Hawaii, but was detained at the airport, stuck in a holding cell, where she was subjected to Champagne, and lobster (locally sourced), then limo-ed back to Taipei, where she was held a political prisoner, in a corner suite of a luxury hotel with private entrance to the pool and sauna. Trump was livid. He handed me a plane ticket to Taipei and told me to take care of the Professor.

I confronted him with the best of American etiquette, "What the hell is going on?"

He laughed, "I got your tariffs right here," he said pointing to Barbi, sitting next to him, smiling.

I demanded he set her free.

"No, no, first you must beg," he said, laughing, "one knee, go, get down and beg." He waited a heartbeat, "It is Taiwanese custom to be humble, gracious, and complimentary to all guests, whether they be rivals, or friends. Your rude and demeaning behavior toward our country was disrespectful, and now you must beg for forgiveness."

"If you touch one hair on her head…"

He laughed, reached over and very daintily touched her hair. She seemed faintly amused.

"You will pay dearly for this…" I started angrily, but I was all too aware that matters had changed. Who held the upper hand?

When informed of this encounter, Trump bade me stay awhile in Taipei. Revenge.

He was running out of people to carry out his vengeance. The FBI, under that -I don't know what he was, Krash the self-improvement infomercial personal injury guy- but under his hapless leadership, between attrition and the ex-dog-walker new-hires, the Bureau had shriveled up like an ED suspect in ice water. The CIA had retreated so far underground, even Moles were bumping into each other. Local police enforcement had scattered success maintaining control, but between chasing after shoplifters and ICE thugs, they were stretched beyond the limits of their job description.

The ugliness was growing. The We the Peepers and the WTFers, with funding from the WCA, in concert with Pro-Taiwan, Ukraine, Anti-ICE hooligans were taking over college campuses, blocking bridges, and creating dissent all over the country. Random riots broke out. As civilian unrest rose, there were massive protests in Charleston, New Orleans, and Winnetka, while those sickos in Portland danced around in Bunny Costumes playing hacky-sack, and naked bike riders chased ICE agents into the Willamette River.

At first, we assumed it was only the Left and their violent Antifa tendencies, but more and more it was rogue ICE and ex-ICE agents who were roaming the streets attacking and pounding on anyone they deemed worthy, especially in those Blue States and sanctuary cities where ICE was virtually outlawed. Trump refused to intervene, but local law enforcement along with WCA controlled National Guard, began 'Operation the Iceman Cometh,' rounding up the rogue ICE-agents en masse. Border control was more and more being enforced by the Mexican military, and pretty soon all old ICE facilities were one-by-one becoming ICE-agent detention centers. With no due process.

As if it weren't already, social media was total anarchy as the vitriol from Right/Left, Blue/Red, was vicious and unrelenting. But when rhetoric turns to bullets, we got a problem. A slew of attempted and some successful assassinations of marginal figures on both sides, left everyone with a horrible sense of vulnerability, and rattled the administration to its core.

When someone took a shot at a judge (missed, thank god) in

Florida, the one responsible for expurgating the word 'slave,' from all textbooks, everyone in the judiciary panicked. Already under constant death threats, the two elder of the SCOTUS-Six abruptly resigned, 'retired', and two others realigned, or at least promised to soften their allegiances, so that Trump no longer had a majority on the Supreme Court. He nominated Donnie Jr. for the highest court, but the laughter was so loud it never made it to the floor for a vote. Every other day Trump would nominate someone, going as far down the chain as Michele Tafoya- all completely ignored. SCOTUS was disarmed.

Mitch is grousing in the corner, muttering something in Spanglish. Maybe a word with him would cheer him up. He looks up in horror at me, "That's when it began," he pokes me in the chest with thumb and index finger, "that damn convoy…why did I let them in the state?!"

No, see that was the problem, you tried your damnedest to keep them out of your state, police, road blocks, you yourself and the Governor stood arm and arm with local cops, demanding them to turn back. Remember? But suddenly the whole state was exploding with sympathy for farmers. And you had no way, legally or physically, to stop them. The convoy started to push through. Joined by the We the Peepers, the radical left descended and that's when you called in the state troopers, they pulled out the rifles, and at your command began shooting, whacking heads, spraying tear gas, throwing protestors to the pavement, handcuffing them. You stood on a platform trying to block the cavalcade, thousands strong, but you, the cops were no use, the vehicles plowed through. You didn't relent. Until you were finally carted off on a gurney.

The convoy continued.

"Tough luck," I say to him, "seems like a state should be able to keep out anyone it wants to, eh?"

He gives me an evil stare, "You're one of them, aren't you?"

I put a hand on his shoulder, "Yes, I'm one of them…just like you."

He nods, his thin lips work into a thin grin, "Yes…we should get us a convoy…" he looks around the yard, up at the towers, the barbed wire, "a convoy would do it."

I leave him alone. At least I gave him some hope.

The two biggest ratings hits in Canada were 'Late Night with the Draft-Dodgers,' and 'Cooking With Antifa,' both clearly anti-American, and both CBC shows streaming around the globe. For an extra poke in the eye, 'Draft-Dodgers' won the Emmy. (Trump's authoritarian rule carried no weight in Hollywood, as nasty NATAS told him to go jump in the Gulf of Mexico). The Canadian pot-shots at us were having their effect. Trump threatened raising the tariffs to 127 % (pull a number out of the hat!), and demanded MLB kick the Toronto Blue Jays out of baseball, right in the middle of a pennant race. The Yankees quickly seconded the motion. Then he declared hockey was no longer legal in America. That last one was a HUGE mistake. 'Take to the ICE,' became the battle-cry of American hockey fans (most of them wearing MAGA hats), waving hockey sticks and throwing puck-size 'buffalo chips' at ICE agents. In Detroit, fans threw octopuses at the ICE detention facility. We lost the hockey vote.

Canada in response, very politely, closed its borders to all American citizens unless they could prove they did not vote for Trump (usually a simple, "Fuck no, I didn't vote for him!" would suffice), then they were allowed in, and given poutine.

A huffy Foxump News aired 'Americans Turned Away from the Border!' videos. One, showing cars denied entry into Canada at Mackinac Island, turned out to be a clip from an old newsreel of a check point in Yugoslavia from 1968. But that didn't undermine the premise. 'Canada hates us,' and only the elite, and DEIs were being allowed in. One clip of a limo full of Hip-Hop artists happily being waved through a barricade, proved to be taken at a red carpet event for the Grammy's. Another showing Mexican bandoleros crossing by horse into Canada was actually ripped from an old John Wayne movie.

A video, which did not make Foxump, went viral, showing an American jumping from a coal barge into the St. Lawrence River, and then leaping from one chunk of large floating ice to another, at least a dozen of them, all the way across the river, where he was pulled ashore by a cheering crowd in Quebec City, at the Plains of Abraham. It was pretty clear it was at best a doctored video, and more likely an AI fake altogether. But as JD likes to say, it doesn't have to be true to make a point. It sure looked cool.

Trump announced he was working on papers to annex Canada, just as soon as he finished proofreading his version of 'The Constitution: Bad News for Modern Man.' He claimed the Army was prepared to march on Montreal and take over the government. This was pretty bad news to the Army. They had already been spun around like a top for the past year, just as they were lacing up their boots to invade Iraq, they were told to 'put on a sweater, you're going to Finland,' 'no, wait, get your diving gear, you're off to Bora Bora.' And now Canada? From the top down, the Army took off their boots, and said, 'No way.'

The Army was not in an accommodating mood. Hogspit had already seen to that. He sent an email to all Army personnel above the level of Private (and 'accidentally' CC'd all Walmart employees), ordering them to send him weekly reports on 1) how many push-ups a day they were doing. 2) The length of their beards. And 3) how many same-sex encounters they witnessed in the shower. The Army responded with a group email signed by some 400 generals sent to Hogspit, and to every media outlet in Western Civilization: 'LOL. GFY.'

One positive came out of it all, as a Walmart employee led everyone with 100 push-ups a day.

The Navy was equally fed-up with Hogspit. He ordered Admirals at every level to take swimming lessons and to compete in weekly swim meets. The losers had to swim extra laps. On a Zoom meeting with the five highest ranking admirals, in which he included his bartender, Bill, he ordered them to surround California with as many aircraft carriers as necessary. When one admiral dryly pointed out that California is surrounded on three sides by land, Hogspit yelled, "You know what I mean! Bill, get me a Stinger." A day later a photo of rubber duckies in a bath tub surrounding a cut-out of California, was posted on the Navy website, with the caption, 'Here you go -Mission Accomplished!'

Li'l Marco is confused. He's not sure why he's here. "They keep saying I was Secretary of State," he laughs, "when did that happen?! I don't remember that…I've never been a secretary…what do I look like, a stenographer…no, that's not me. If I was such a big shot Secretary of State, why wasn't I working on the treaties with Prussia and Monongahela, or negotiating salmon spawns in Alaska. No, they got me confused with someone else."

"Well, for one thing," I point out, "you went to Russia to convince Putin to accept Ukraine's full surrender…"

"Putin? No way. That guy's out of his mind, he's a murderer, I'd end up falling out a window somewhere. Hell no, I ain't getting involved. I did talk to one of his secretaries. I thought 'hey, secretary, that's my level,' her name was Svetlana, she was making tea for the boss, and I saw her slip something in it, like a pill or something, and she told me, 'Here, take this in to Vlad, he could really use this.' *Do svidaniya*, baby, I was out of there lickety-split. No way, Secretary of State? Not for this kid."

"Weren't you the one that ordered tanks from that Hungarian tyrant to try to block the convoy from getting to DC?"

"No, that was a mix-up, most of the tanks didn't work, they were old decommissioned Russian tanks from World War II, and we got them for a song…but I had nothing to do with that dictator… just wanted his recipe for goulash…no, no…I never even met him."

"Look, Marco, ole boy, you were up to your ears in diplomatic fuck-ups."

He suddenly looks at the ground, nods, uncommittedly, "Yeah…damn ears…"

The EU rid its countries of American military presence. First, Germany closed the base at Stuttgart, then all others within their borders, followed by Poland, Italy, Spain, and the United Kingdom. American bases and garrisons all over Europe were shuttered. America's once mighty military presence in Europe was gone, replaced by the lone presence of the almighty tourist dollar, which thanks to tariffs, was worth about 2 cents on the Euro.

Out of nowhere, Trump announced he was going to regulate Crypto, and in fact, had already begun doing so, behind the Fed's back, so no one had any say in the matter. Except Trump. He set limits on cashing out, put a ceiling on gains, added penalties and or royalties for every trade, to be paid to him, through his rigged financial company. Control fell to a new government watch-dog (Eric). The Crypto community flipped out. Financially stung banks, public companies, big-tech moguls, my cousin Jimmy, everyone fled from Crypto like it was Agent Orange. They closed their accounts at a huge loss, and sent speculative money crashing back to virtual worthlessness. Wall Street was furious, and sank Crypto-completely. The reader board read '0.'

The Bitcoin Bust was on.

Afterwards, my cohorts would be found muttering, 'No, not me, I never put a dime in Bitcoin…O, maybe just a pittance, just to stay in the game.' Bullshit. They lost millions. I know.

Like a gambler cashing in his chips just before the joint gets raided, Trump converted millions worth of Crypto currency into memecoins bearing his image, but alas, they were worth less than the alloyed silver they were pressed in. He was stuck with a dozen pirate's chests full of worthless doubloons.

Taiwan got rescued. In Ukraine, that little Gecko steadfastly refused to give up either his right or his left arm to Putin. Brazil scuttled Trump's tariffs by funneling goods through Saudi Arabia, which can't live without coffee and hookah. Brazilian coffee was more popular and cheaper than ever. Russia and China loomed over the US like two vultures waiting for road kill.

The EU thumbed their nose at us as our economy began to crumble under the weight of the Crypto crash.

Did we, the Faithful, lose faith? No, we were too far down the path with Trump. We could only hope there was some magic left in that hat of his. Maybe he had been bluffing, now he would start negotiating with everyone! After all, he was the Master of the Art of the Deal. Wasn't he? Besides, if the end were coming, what else were we to do? Go down with the ship.

The Mexican military moved in on Texas, for 'security' reasons, as the Texas National Guard was stranded in Idaho, trying to quell what was thought to be a potato uprising, but as luck would have it was just harvest time. Ted was on holiday in Oaxaca. No one seemed too alarmed. The Texas legislature, not known for having a spine, scampered down the marbled steps, filing out onto Congress Ave., leaving Mexican-Americans, largely third generation citizens, and Mexican Nationals, some legislators from Chihuahua, to take over the legislature. They drew up new rules of order, drafted laws, and re-established the supremacy of the Texas Bill of Rights. Austin's Sixth St. was rocking night and day with a mix of blues and mariachi music, as smoke filled the air from the dozens of BBQ joints, and people danced in the streets until dawn, celebrating Texas's return to the jurisdiction of Mexico.

In the middle of it all Trump fought back as only he can, in ALL CAPS. Every twenty minutes, each post sounding more and more desperate, preposterous, and alarming, 'DON'T MAKE ME PUSH THE BUTTON!'

The We the Peepers and WCA kept the lawsuits coming like ping pong balls, and Trump had no support from SCOTUS. Partly out of fear for their lives, and fear of retribution from Trump, the Supreme Court declared itself on indefinite leave, refusing to hear any more cases. Every judge on record was either postponing judgements, or hiding under desks and in closets, leaving only those courageous judges to continue handing out rulings against Trump's demands for military action against the American people.

The government came to a standstill.

The tractors, combines, flatbeds, and the pitchfork wielding farmers had come to DC and blocked 1-495. All interchanges became checkpoints, especially at the Springfield interchange where traffic was allowed to continue, albeit with stoppages and potty breaks, but for long suffering commuters of the Beltway, nothing new there.

Trump declared the Country in a State of Emergency. He put out on social media that the mid-terms were canceled indefinitely. Republicans in Congress got antsy. They'd supported him on everything so far, but halting elections? They more than balked, worse than balked, they went on indefinite recess. Trump suspended all commercial trade with Canada, Mexico, and Liberia (?!), and was preparing to deploy the military to recapture Texas, and take over the sanctuary cities. All at this point, threats as empty as a beggar's Crypto cup.

Congress was depleted, with Republicans hiding behind pillars and in restrooms, the Dems flooded the floors with speeches and declarations, but without a two-thirds majority they couldn't override Trump's State of Emergency. So they bickered amongst themselves.

Blue and Purple States around the country took charge of everything within their own borders, aligning themselves with the WCA, which already had an office in Congress and was holding daily briefings, sending out memos, threatening to secede, or if worse came to worst, go to war to take over the federal government. Red States polished their guns, and made sure their bunker was well stocked with canned beef.

Once Trump declared a State of Emergency, the army took the 'everyman for himself' approach. Defying Trump they re-commissioned numerous generals and Pentagon officials that Trump and Hogspit had railroaded out. In particular, ex-Chief of Staff, General Milkey, the one who had (regrettably) accompanied Trump across Lafayette Square to a church, where the President sanctified a copy of 'Gone With the Wind,' mistaking it for the Bible. Hopping mad, The General turned against Trump. Once back in power, Trump did everything he could to emasculate The General. Fired him, revoked his security clearance, and threatened to bring charges against him. But Trump's team of Keystone lawyers couldn't find a legal way to break through the Invisible Shield Biden had put around The General.

I've noticed this about people, when you take savage revenge on someone, and then they have the opportunity to take vengeance in return, they're not going to be in a very forgiving mood. But The General was at least gracious about it. He took away Trump and Hogspit's keys to the Pentagon, and blocked their access to all military texts, emails, and Tik Tok. In a State of Emergency, Milkey claimed, the military was obligated to take whatever means necessary to secure control.

Can he do that? Trump sought counsel from his son-by-law, Jaded Krushner, but he'd been replaced by a mannequin years ago. His new attorney that he met at a McDonald's, looked through the Bad News Constitution and advised Trump Milkey was probably right, but he should sue him anyway. And did he want fries with that? Trump decided to let The General have his way, after all, he had an army standing behind him.

Trump now had no military, SCOTUS was on 'indefinite temporary recess,' local governments were all fending for themselves, the WCA, WTFers, and We the Peepers were in control of social media and entertainment, wielding most of the power over the popular imagination, and gaining more and more control of the government.

The shit had hit the fan

Everyone on our side of the aisle began abandoning ship, from the valet parking attendant to the majority Speaker of the House. Li'l Marco was in Puerto Rico applying for a driver's license so he could run for governor, Ted was in Machu Picchu. Tubby was coaching North Carolina, Empty G was home binge watching 'My Little Margie.' But like Laurel and Hardy, JD and Trump remained true to one another.

Leaving the radical left Dems to run Congress, and while they had no majority to vote on anything, they managed to push through a new law that in States of Emergency (thanks, Donald) they can reduce the Majority Rule to those who were present. It was known as the tautology rule, it's only a rule, because we say it's a rule. They slapped every sanction they could on Trump, impeached him again, and again. But they had no authority. It was all gas, no engine. Nothing they said was enforceable.

The only group with any real power at that point at the federal level was the military, and unlike a good ole-fashioned Bolshevik or Sandinista military coup, they simply stood back and watched. Referee if need be, but that's it, like traffic guards at a school crossing. They were as much keeping an eye on Russia and China as Portland, Oregon. But Milkey made it clear, they were not going to interfere with a change of power.

We were sunk.

Something is afoot in the compound, more guards are arriving, and there seems to be a general hubbub. Ted points out the Day of the Dead celebration is coming up, maybe they're going to put on a show for us. "You'll really enjoy it," he tells everyone, "the Mexicans go all out. It's like Christmas!" Okay. I doubt it, but something definitely is going on. These don't look like theater people, with their guns and uniforms.

Jorge is tight-lipped, "I don't know," he says when I ask, "everything seems normal to me…" but he wears a grin that says otherwise.

"Should I prepare myself for a flogging and water torture?"

His smile broadens, "You should always prepare yourself for everything, amigo."

JD was seen all around DC, his stupid helmeted head poking out the top of an old Russian tank rumbling down Pennsylvania Ave., and spinning around the National Mall, reminding everyone of Dukakis.

Not the inspirational image we were looking for at that moment. It became apparent Trump no longer had the authority to carry out any of his threats. His cabinet of mice had scuttled beneath refrigerators, and into the crawl-space. Hogspit hid in Dick Cheney's Underground Bunker.

Our First Lady, the Goddess of Ice, Melatonia, was the first to bolt the scene altogether. After her appearance at the inauguration wearing a frying pan on her head, she had pretty much faded into the wallpaper at the White House. Every now and again emerging for a photo-op with that frying pan on her head (a fashion statement that, bewilderingly, never quite caught on). Why such a beauty would make herself look so stupid, was beyond speculation. We all had trophy wives, and we knew their level of intellect. They can appear to be bright without being sharp. But Melatonia was sharp. She knew her only asset was her beauty, and if that were fading, cover it up with a skillet. And I'll tell you what, she wasn't about to take the fall for anyone. Least of all some two-bit player huckster on a one-way street to Loserville. When the JD hit the fan, she took to her suite inside the Power Tower in New York City. Protestors kept the building under constant siege, largely because of the neon Wordle 'Trump' glaring down on them, but also in the slim chance that the man himself might step out of a limo affording them the opportunity for whizzing a brick past his head. It was worth the wait. Though at that point the likelihood of him leaving the White House or Mar-a-Lego was pretty slim.

Melatonia was not stupid. She might have been vapid, shamelessly insipid, regally out-of-touch, but not stupid. She managed to escape by disguising herself as a washer woman, stripping her face of makeup, smudging her cheeks, brushing dark circles under her eyes, coloring a couple of teeth black, and wrapping her head in a dirty babushka, and then, dressed like a chambermaid, just strolled out the side door pushing a basket of dirty laundry with the rest of the night staff. And while the duped protesters cheered and raised cups, shouting 'Hoozah' for the proletariat, 'We the people!' Embracing the moment, Melatonia raised an arm in the Jan. 6 salute. The crowd cheered. The left-libs had their Proletariat Hero, the charwoman! She broke from her 'co-workers,' crossed over to Central Park, walked to a waiting limo, was whisked off to Kennedy, and waving her Melantiska Knaja passport, caught a red-eye to Amsterdam, where she partied on the canals for a week, and then took a private jet to Slovenia. Good riddance.

The last anyone saw of RFCK Jr., was after he left Mar-a-Lego, where he and Trump pledged allegiance to each other, and toasted with fetid water on the rocks. The rocks having come from a coal mine in Kentucky. They vowed to fight like hell to keep their people free… of vaccines, health care…and to keep this government intact. RFCK then gathered his entourage to go out inspecting the swamps of the bayou, where he was looking to build a winter home. It was coming on dark and as he stood with the local sheriff pointing to the alligators, lying still as stone in the murk, their eyes just above water, glaring at the humans, looking as if they were looking over the menu. A sheriff was explaining to RFCK the natural habits of the common swamp alligator, their nesting places, how much they eat a day, and what their diets consisted of. "Humans?" RFCK inquired. The sheriff nodded, "Sometimes." By all accounts it was at that moment, RFCK staring out across the swamp in the gloaming, with the caw of southern crows in the trees, the breeze pushing the rushes back and forth, without a word he began to undress. No one knew what to do. He took off his shoes, stripped down naked, and before anyone could even begin to imagine what was going on, he stepped towards the banks through the reeds and dangling branches of cypress trees, waded into the swamp, as he got knee deep in the gunky waters he stretched himself him out and began floating away quietly, without a ripple. The alligators slapped their tails, their heads craned above the surface, and they slowly began to move, but not at RFCK, instead they approached the shoreline, some five or six of them formed a circle around RFCK as if protecting him, as he drifted further out into the swamp. The sheriff raised a rifle and took a shot at one of the gators, who did a quick slashing tail-spin, seemingly unhurt, but agitated, which roused the ire of the other gators, who began to rise and come out of the water. The sheriff and the entourage ran off. Darkness was falling. They never looked back.

A photo emerged on the internet days later, a grainy photo of swampy waters, and far out from shore, a human head protruding up to its nose, perfectly still, eyes peering out, unblinking. If it were a doctored photo, and most experts insisted it was not, it was better done than Sasquatch. But everyone agreed, it sure looked like RFCK Jr.

The dream was over. Trump was caught running up the ramp of his newly outfitted 400 million dollar bribe, the 'Fortress in the Sky,' trying to make his escape to Qatar, but the plane was unable to get off the ground, as the prince who gifted the plane to Trump, forgot give him the passcode, and no one could get the door open.

WAPO gleefully pieced together Trump's attempted escape in an animated video with diagrams and text depicting him as a plump blue Lego in the White House. He crawls out from under the Resolute Desk, and with little red dots tracing his footsteps, he runs out of the Oval Room, down the corridor towards the East Wing, but, uh-oh, it's gone, he ducks into a closet re-emerges wearing a wig, races down the corridor where a chambermaid tosses him a burger, which he swallows in one bite, then slides butt-first down the rail to the first floor, out onto the balcony, he leaps over the rail onto his Bouncy Castle, does a couple mid-air back flips, jumps into a golf cart and careens out the gates toward the National Mall where JD is waiting for him in a white Bronco, and together they race off down Constitution Ave., speeding, taking turns on two wheels. They get pulled over by the National Guard who demand to see their papers. Trump, wearing a long floppy wig and lipstick, and JD in clown make-up, promise they'll behave, and blowing kisses, speed off, weaving in and out of traffic on 695, and soon are being chased by five cop cars, but JD hits a button, and suddenly the

Bronco sprouts rotors on top, and they go airborne, and glide across the night sky to land on the tarmac at Andrews Airforce Base, and as they get out, Trump shoves JD to the ground and runs to the plane where a soldier, half-assed salutes him, and relays information that they can't get into the plane. They're waiting for a return text from the Prince for the passcode, but he's stuck in traffic on 495, seems there was some road-rage incident, and Trump screams in anger, but then sees General Milkey with a couple dozen troops marching towards him, and runs up the ramp, and pounds on the door to the plane, screaming, big teardrops fly out his eyes like sparks off a firecracker. Trump is escorted off.

Bozos tried to kill the piece, but he had lost control of WAPO's editorial staff when he got stuck in space (the landing gear fell off his Red Origin space ship and the pieces were floating tauntingly in orbit around the space ship). WAPO's leftist-radical editors, all three of them, booted out all the right wing commentators and MAGA political cartoonists, and ran nothing but caustic lib pieces calling for Trump's impeachment. The rogue editors also began live streaming Bozos, circling the earth in low atmosphere, with his 'guests,' Kid Rock, Kevin Hart, and Foxump's Lora Hangaham. Bozos can be seen leaning forward shouting, "Alexa, cancel WAPO's story on Trump's escape…"

"I'm sorry I don't know how to do that, consult the Alexa App available in your…"

"Alexa…no!"

Kevin Hart is explaining to Kid Rock, "They told us we're going up, never said anything about coming back down…"

Kid Rock looks panicked, and a bit seasick. Hangaham is crouched in a fetal position up against a wall.

Bozos shouts, "Alexa, Just cancel the damn paper…Kevin will you shut up."

"Would you like to upgrade to full 24-hour assistance for Amazon Spaceship Premium Maintenance for $29.95 a month…just say 'Alexa…'"

"No, Alexa, just cancel the damn paper…"

"I'm afraid I don't know that one, but here's some music by Leufey…."

Kevin Hart could be heard saying, "So you bring black folk up here just to leave them in space?"

Kid Rock shouts, "Alexa, don't play Leufey, for godssake…I'm already sick…"

"Hello, I hear a new voice I don't recognize, what is your name?"

"Kid Rock."

"Hi, Kid, so that I can get to know you better, tell me about some of the things you enjoy."

"Threesomes, orgies, beer…"

"Kid, is there an adult I can talk to…"

"Alexa, it's me," Bozos whines, "I just want you to stop all editions, print and online from coming out!"

"I'm afraid I can't help you with that, please consult the Alexa App…"

"Alexa…stop."

"I shoulda listened to Lebron...don't go up there with that bald billionaire...wait, I said, you're a bald billionaire..."

The screen went blank at that point, and as far as anyone knows, Bozos and crew are still circling the Earth, and occasionally, when the Red Origin passes over Three Mile Island, people have been known to catch a radio signal, you can faintly hear Kevin Hart, "What if I push this blue button, what'll that do?...."

"Don't touch anything!"

Royalty has come to visit us, and I hope it's a short stay. Donnie Jr. is our new guest of honor. He thinks he is here to lecture us, make us fall in line. He is immediately disabused of that notion, as he is strapped to the tether pole in the center of the yard, which interrupted a perfectly good game between Tubby and I, as my serve was killer, running a string of aces. In fact, I think he purposely had Junior strapped to the pole so he wouldn't look like the loser he is.

Donnie fearlessly, or stupidly, begins haranguing everyone, and when a guard comes too close he shouts, "Hey, you can't just strap me here in this shithole country! Where's my due process?"

The guard looks at him astonished, "You've got to be fucking kidding," he says "now, YOU want due process. Tell that to my cousin, Maria." he shakes his head disgustedly and walks away.

Donnie glances around for someone to yell at when he spots me, "Hey you, you getting all the soft pillows and pink Champagne you need here?"

"Shut up dickhead," I said, much to the glee of some, and dismay of others, "you're the reason we're all here, you and your big fat mouth..."

"Oh, and not you? Judas!"

A guard strolls up to Donnie, puts the barrel of his automatic up against his cheek, and brushes the beard softly, making it relatively clear this kind of exchange is forbidden in the yard.

"Have a good day dickhead," I walk away.

"Rot in hell, traitor."

I am not a traitor. Nor am I an informant. I don't betray. But I do have this awful character flaw, under extreme pressure, when cornered by absolutes and directness, I can't help but tell the truth. I'm good at evasiveness and fudging, but when it comes right down to it, I must tell the truth.

As everyone on our side of the aisle had absconded from the premises, the 'bipartisan' tribunal was composed mostly of radical-libs. They were quick and decisive. Blue State Wide Mouth chaired the panel, and began the questioning of me, at first in broad, innocuous seeming enquiries; what I thought about my relationship with the president, how much he relied on me, and me him, the trust level between us. My answers were evasive, dodging, a couple 'I don't knows.' And then he came to the escalator incident. I was to meet with the President of Taiwan, our final encounter. He was coming down the escalator with his wife for a meeting with my delegation, when the escalator stopped suddenly and the President took a nasty fall. Few broken bones, but he's okay. Now. After a month in the hospital. His wife was unhurt.

"Did the president ever bring up in your presence, his own misadventure with the escalator?"

"Yes, quite often."

"Was he upset by it?"

"Yes, very."

"Did he ever say, 'I'm glad the escalator wasn't going down?'"

"I don't recall those specific words."

"Did he ever indicate he was aware that if the escalator had stopped going down it could have done serious harm to him…and his wife?"

"That's a vague assertion…I don't recall any reference of that nature."

"So…he never made you think he was aware of the danger of a fall down the escalator?"

"I think we all have that fear…"

"That's not what I'm asking."

"Then….maybe something along those lines…a toss-away comment…"

Then Blue State pulls out a large photo of a long and steep escalator. "Do you recognize this photo?" No, not the photo, I couldn't say I did. "Did the President mention that in your meeting with the President of Taiwan, he would be descending this particular elevator?" I don't know why he would. "Did the president give you a specific order to stop the escalator when he was near the top?"

"No sir."

"O, look at that," he leans back, sarcastically, "a non-waffling answer… thank you. We're making headway. Then can you answer this, yes or no, in your own mind, did you think the president suggested that if you could arrange to have the escalator stop suddenly it would bring possible damage, considerable, severe damage, to the president of Taiwan? Yes or no."

I pause, grinding the gears in my head.

As I'm not answering, Blue State closes in on me, "You are a student of history?"

"Yes, sir."

Then he says slowly, so as to let his words sink in, "You must be familiar with Henry II, and Thomas Beckett, Archbishop of Canterbury?"

"Sounds familiar…"

Looking down at his notes, he goes on, "'Will no one rid me of this turbulent priest?'" He is quoting an angry Henry II blurting out those words, what seemed to his henchman to be a command, or permission, to assassinate the Archbishop of Canterbury, Thomas Beckett. A deed they almost immediately carried out. "Recall the incident?"

"Yes, sir. I do."

"Thank you. Yes or no, did you believe Trump, maybe in a toss-away comment, was ordering you to bring harm to the president of Taiwan? Yes or no."

I am not a traitor. I do not betray the trust of others. I am not a Judas. But I cannot lie

Elections across America are on Tuesday. As scheduled. We petitioned for absentee ballots, but the Mexicans with grim humor point out convicted felons cannot vote in the election, and besides we are now property of the state of Chihuahua, Mexico.

"And as you are illegals here, you may not vote in our elections either."

It is the Day of the Dead. The yard is surrounded by sugar skulls, brightly colored, and smiling, on poles of varying heights, like tiki torches. Candles, hanging flower baskets, are placed at stations around the yard. The mariachi band and dancers, have been practicing all day. We've been kept out of the yard so as not to interfere with rehearsal and set-up. All this for us? Day of the Dead? Not sure I like it. Jorge tells me the festivities won't begin until it's completely dark. And he says it is a good omen if I live through the night.

It's not quite dark when they let us out into the yard. I spy a female, standing by the gate, American, among three female guards. Takes a moment, but I recognize her. The good reverend, PaulaPaula, spiritual guide to the Universe. And to Trump. Looks a bit different, with all the bleach blond washed out, and designer dresses and high heeled shoes swapped out for prison garb. She must've gotten special dispensation to be on this side. I take a measured risk and stroll slowly towards her. The guards give me a glance, but not threateningly, so I go up to her, "Is that really you?"

PaulaPaula smiles, "Hey you." Good. She forgot my name.

The guards seem okay, so I continue, "Are you here for the festivities? I hear the big show begins at nightfall."

She looks at me quizzically, "Then you know about?…" she pauses.

"About what?" Wait. My brain goes 'click.' She's his spiritual advisor. His dumbshit of a son is here. Beefed up security. Could this be the moment we've all been waiting for?

If it is, I won't spoil the surprise for everyone else. If not, none's the wiser. "Gonna be a big night," I say. I get the feeling the female guards do not understand English. But I've been fooled before, so I'm cautious.

"I hope so," she says, guardedly.

"Are you here for the spiritual part of the festivities?"

"In a manner of speaking," she says.

Yes, now I'm sure of it. I can almost feel his presence. Just as I'm thinking myself so smart, a kind of gulp of surprise goes up, a bit of tittering, and I see people pointing up at the sky. A string of lights is passing overhead, from the northeast, slowly, very slowly, forming a message.

The reverend takes my arm, points up…"It's a message from God!"

"No," I assure her, "it's just EVlon…" He uses his strings of tiny satellites for 'sky writing,' sending mean nasty notes to us heathen down below. The first was to Trump as he was being escorted out of the courtroom, 'So long, sucker.'

"I don't have my glasses, what does it say…." she squints.

"'Go fuck yourself.'"

She nods, knowingly, "He should be down here with the rest of us," then sighs, "maybe there is no God after all." She turns her head, the guards have motioned to her, "There's my cue," she says, and steps away.

Darkness is complete. The crowd is antsy. A sense of exaggerated drama is prevalent. Or is it just the lunch burritos? The mariachi band starts playing a frenetic festive tune. The dancers begin twirling their hoop squirts, and circling one another, and then with a loud crunch, the gates begin to part. The rebar creaks and groans, the barbed wire wiggles, as the large gates swing open into the yard. JD is prancing around like a satyr tossing flower petals in the air. PaulaPaula is kneeling, head bowed, folded hands above her head. And then the nose of a black truck pokes through the opening. It rumbles into the yard, people spread out making way for it, caught fleetingly in the headlights. The truck creeps forward till it is inside and the gates begin to close. The truck backs up, and does a slow 360 turn. The bed of the truck now faces us, and we see a figure, his back against the cabin. It's him. There's a hush. The truck backs up to the center of the compound. He's there, draped in a large toga that spreads out like a parachute in enormous folds half way across the truck. Hanging from his neck, is a bright red, what appears to be either a noose or a leash, or perhaps a neck tie, and slithers down in a tangle among the folds of the parachute. I'm sure I wasn't the only one thinking, Jabba the Hutt. Everyone looks around apprehensively. Do we applaud? Scream? We all just stand there, glancing around to see what others would do. I have the feeling if one person were to applaud, everyone would. Or if one person threw a rock, we all would.

The guards, a dozen or so, position themselves around the truck, automatics at hip position. The band stops playing. The dancers whirl off to the side. Trump sits there, an orange halo on his head.

As I look on, what I see is a figure, once the most powerful person on Earth, now bound, feeble, ignoble. He could as easily have been a nice guy who brought joy and happiness to the world, a presidential Santa Claus. He could've rewarded people, spoke highly of them, gave them credit for all their achievements, he could have developed a cure for cancer. He could've gone around the world shaking hands with world leaders, small and large, rejoicing in their togetherness and shared will to solve all the world's problems, to resolve all differences, he could have brought peace and unity. And now there he sits. Alone. A guard reaches up and hands him a microphone, the one we use for karaoke night, it crackles and spits. He takes it daintily between his fingers, puts it to his lips, and lifting his chin, all three of them, the man who could've been the Man above all other Men, looks out across his quiet supplicants, "You're all going to pay for this," he snarls. And my reverie comes to an end.

Obviously angry, he says something nasty to the guards, and there's a commotion, as we wait, someone hands him another microphone. "Can anybody hear me?" he snaps, "what a pissant operation, shithole country ..." he mutters, the microphone crackles, goes off for a second, then back on, "There," he sneers, and states flatly, "your Daddy's home." There's actually a hand clap or two, but mostly silence. "Nice place you got here," he surveys the crowd, the compound, the guards, "do any of these people," he indicates the guards around his stage, "understand English?"

"No, we're too stupid," one of the guards calls out, "speak your English, we won't understand a word you say. No one ever does. Say what you want."

Trump starts to say something that starts with an 'F' and ends with a 'you,' but after a pause says, "This a great place you got, nice and secure. You know who built this, don't you? We did, in six months, look at that beautiful wall, American know-how..."

A guard shouts out, "No...we Mexicans built it in two months, amigo!"

"With American dollars," he retorts, "American design, American know-how, American engineering, you couldn't have laid a single brick without our..."

"No amigo, if you Americans tried to build this we'd all be standing in a pile of shit right now, cuz nothing would've gotten done.."

"Will somebody shut him up, I didn't come here to be yelled at by an illegal..."

"You're the illegal here," a guard snaps, while the muzzle of his rifle rises above the crowd, and a quick burst of shots ring out. We try to duck for cover, but sardines have a difficult time moving in a tin can. No further shots are fired. The muzzle waivers.

Trump is crouching, several chins buried in his chest. Then gathers himself, in the microphone, "Go on, fire away, I already took one bullet for my country…I can take another."

The muzzle of the rifle lowers, aims at Trump. His eyes go big, blood drains from his face. The rifle is drawn down and disappears.

He breathes deeply, "This is a dangerous place," deep-breath, pause, "But I'm among friends…right? Used-to-be friends. Are they treating you good here? You look well fed…"

"It's the chicken tacos," someone yells out.

Trump just glares. He tips his head like a large ball has rolled from one side of his brain to the other, "Tacos," he says, "you pig." JD is leaning on a fender of the truck, holding the basket of flower petals, idly watching his idol. Then he mindlessly sticks his hand in the basket, pulls out a fistful of petals and stuffs them in his mouth. He chews, and watches.

"Yeah, your Daddy is here, and he's mad. All you…where's your loyalty now," he indicates himself in the parachute and the leash, "all I've done for you…So loyal to me, kissed the ring, didn't you, and now… who stood up for me? I who did everything for you, did you stand up for me? Here you are, you hate me, the one who gave you all this power…"

We're looking around at one another, 'Hey, nice power, thanks.'

"Say it in all caps," Geetz shouts. He's become somewhat indignant and pretty negative since his failed escape.

Trump ignores him. "Makes sense," he looks down at the guards, "we'd end up in Mexico. After all I've done for this country. I was your best friend, I made this country what it is. Hey, I ended the Hispanic wars, got rid of all the drug dealers, I ended all the wars down here in South America…"

"Central America," some cartographer wannabe in the crowd points out.

"Whatever…it was a mess until I cleaned it up, I did that with one phone call, saved your asses…and did I get any thanks for that? No, your president could have called." There's some grumbling among the guards, and wiggling of rifles, "It's okay, we've got a good relationship, me and your president, he's good guy, he likes me a lot…we met, I don't know, I think it was a summit, didn't have much time to talk, but I know he liked me, I could just tell, and I like him, I think we'll get along really well…"

"Our president, Claudia, is a woman, amigo…"

"What, when did that happen?" he didn't show any alarm. He never does, "oh, right, I was thinking of that other fellow, that Argentine guy…I saved his country, too. Never mind, we have a good relationship, me and your president, we're gonna work together, me and Mexico, and when I get back in power, we'll join forces and make North America great again….kick out that wasteland tundra Canook, useless bunch of socialists, but Mexico, yeah we've got a good relationship….we share a lot. You guys got a great country here. We sent all your illegals back home for you…hey, if you come to our country and get involved with bad things, we send you back to your homeland, so you can be good citizens, work hard, and give back to the local economy, that's been our goal all along. I'm helping Mexico, and you should be more grateful, no one has done more for Mexico than me. I'm very popular with the common people, everyone in America knows, and now here…ask the people on the street, they know me, they like me, where's Li'l Marco, is he here, he'll tell you…"

"Right here, boss!"

"…shut up. When they told me I was coming here, I said fine, great…I want to look my people in the face, in your blood-shot eyes…see what betrayal really looks like."

"Not me, boss…"

"Will you shut up…that's the thanks I get…tell you what, when I get back in power, it's going to be two months, in two months, we're working on it, I got the votes, I got the backing, everyone wants me back, I'll be back in power in two months, and you know where you'll be? Right here…where you belong…things'll be different when I get back in…"

Suddenly there's a commotion and Trump stops, someone yells, "Streaker!" The whole yard breaks out into laughter as U-Hawley, buck naked, goes running behind Trump, stops, and gives him the big January 6 salute. But not with his fist. Another part of his anatomy. Marco claps his hands. We all cheer, and U-Hawley waves and disappears into the crowd.

"That's it, that's what I'm talking about," he points to the vanished streaker, "whackos…when I get out of here, when I'm back on the throne, I am going to wreak such havoc on all of you, you think you got it bad now, you'll wish you were dead when you see what I've got in store for you, yes, the wheels are turning right now, I got people out there, good people, loyal people, we're working on it, and in two weeks we'll be back in power, two weeks and, everyone of you…" and then either he just spots me in the crowd, or has been saving his best for me, "You…you are the worst! you will go down in history with Eggs

Benedict as the biggest traitor in the world…"

"Stop it, you're making us hungry," Geetz yells out.

"I made this the strongest nation on earth, I took you in, gave you a piece of the action …you do this to me." He looks around disdainfully, and as some of us are starting to titter, he looks up to see the sky writing, coming now from the south. He tries to shake a fist at it, but as he can't get his arm up, his ire goes up instead, "O, and I made you too, you cheap used car salesman, you're going to be the first to go down, you snake…" At least we agree on something. "When I get back in power, and it won't be long, I promise, I don't know yet…maybe I'll come back for some of you, but, maybe I won't. We'll see. I don't know yet…in two months, no more, we're working on it. I did it before. When I took over, this country was dead…"

"How dead was it?" Someone yells out.

Trump ignores the interruption, "…this country was dead, the economy was the worst in world, worst it's ever been, immigrants, illegals overran the country, sanctuary cities were just drug dealing Antifa hideouts, my good people were thrown in jail…while terrorists roamed the streets, everywhere, and in six months, that's how long it took me, the worst mess this country has ever been in, six months, and I got everything in shape…I brought back prosperity, peace, all over the world, I ended wars, I can't even count how many wars I ended, and now….this. It's all gone to hell. This country is dead again."

"How dead is it?" someone again yells.

"So dead, we elected him President," another shouts out.

"I didn't come here to be heckled by idiots…" Trump snaps.

"Then why did you come? Vacation?"

"Hey, I was the hardest working president ever, look it up, no president has worked harder than me, ever, no one…"

As he's droning on, I notice a yellow glow, a light from behind him, a heavenly beam shines down, and suddenly rising above the skulls into the night against the backdrop of razors, wires, floodlights, and flowers, colorful dresses, is a figure, ethereal, shrouded in blue light, it is a vision, The Miller, with his death mask, blank eyes, passionless, and empty visage, his arms held out as if granting grace or pronouncing a death sentence to those below, and as he rises a voice cries out, "Come my children…come! The time is now…." though his thin lips do not move, the voice emanates from some ethereal mist, "Come, my children, come! Rise, rise with me…"

PaulaPaula is on her knees, weeping, lamenting, "It's the Rapture! Behold, it's the Rapture!" she cries out. Her arms are held high and for just a moment I think she's going to ascend with him, but she is stuck in the dust, with the rest of us.

The Miller rises far above us, then the beam of light flickers, the light is extinguished, he rises and rises, and then in a burst of flame and smoke, separated only by a beam of light declaring, "Go fuck yourself," he rises, dissipates, and then disappears.

Oddly, Trump has not broken his rant, he prattles on uninterrupted, and PaulaPaula's arms are still held above the crowd, "The rapture has come!" she moans. The rapture has come and apparently gone, and nobody noticed. Her voice rings hollow. Trump only pauses for a second. Maybe to catch his breath, and kicks into a new string of his amazing accomplishments, made America great again, ended wars, saved lives, freed people, etc.

I look over at PaulaPaula, she is now standing listening to Trump. Is it possible we're the only two who saw it? Did I really see it?

Trump rambles on, "….my Big Beautiful Bill will live on, when I come back…" until someone yells out,

"You're not coming back, you've been impeached and impounded."

"Biggest witch hunt in history. None of that was legal, and when I'm back in power, we're going to hunt down every liberal leftist responsible, put them behind bars. I'm not going to play games, we'll welcome back Old Mexico, we belong together, we've always been one country, we'll be the greatest power this world has ever seen, greater than Rome, greater than the Trojan Horses, greater than the Pyramids…The people are crying for me to come back, we're working on it, two months, I'll be back in office, and I'll fix everything, first day, put everything back where it belongs, I'm the only one who can fix it, we'll get Texas back," he points up at the sky, where the lights still blink their message, "yeah, he'll get his, him and his AI buddies, they're destroying everything, Texas, San Francisco, a zombie, druggie ghost town, and New York City, my city, forget it, it's in ruins, run by terrorists…and Portland…Portland…streets filled with garbage, cars on fire, abandoned buildings, armed Antifa roaming the streets, it's a shame, I had that city cleaned up, I brought the military in, they tried to stop me, but I did it, and saved that city, now it's worse than ever, but I'll fix it. Bring in the military, I'm working with them right now, send in troops, like I did with Chicago, DC, Memphis, I had those cities free and clean and prosperous, no one can do what I did, I got us out of the pandemic, worst health crisis since the Blue Bonnet plague, that was me, made us the healthiest country in the world, ask anybody, greatest economy in four hundred years, world peace, I ended seventeen wars, prices are lower than they've been in this century, that was me…I'm a humble guy, but without me…"

A shrill voice comes screaming out from over the other side of the wall, "Liar!"

Everyone stands stock still, sardines not moving in the tin, looking at each other, what should we do? Laugh? Yell back?

She's over on her side of the wall, screeching with laughter, in the dark, sliced through by skulls with flaming eyeballs, the flutter of marigold flower petals sprinkling in the breeze across over the yard, Trump in the middle, striking a pose, I think reenacting his ear shot pose, but he looks helpless. Then Li'l Marco, laughs loudly and claps his hands, and everyone starts clapping along, and the mariachi band strikes up a light Calypso number, the dancers swirl their hoops, then suddenly we all start doing the Trump dance, just moving in place, all smiling at one another, rolling our hands, swaying our hips. Tucker walks out and to everyone's surprise, does the robot dance. He's actually pretty good. Trump sits stunned, mouth agape, I think he's trying to say something but no one can hear, as we're all smiles and dancing and looking up into the sky, to God's message, and there we are dancing, not sure we can keep it up for 39 minutes, when the voice cries out again, "Liar!"

Someone yells back, maybe it's me, "You tell him, Empty G!"

FIN!